Dear...

AMATSUKA MOE

10 TH ANNIVERSARY PHOTOBOOK

SPEED
LIMIT
25

SPEED
LIMIT
25

25

25

25

TONY ROMA'S
FAMOUS FOR RIBS

BUD LIGHT

BUD LIGHT

BUD LIGHT

BUD LIGHT
BAR

BUD LIGHT

らぶぱら
天使もえ

welcom

welcome

3

are
BEAUTIFU
if you
LOVE
T H E M

AMATSUKA MOE

10 TH ANNIVERSARY PHOTOBOOK

Artist: AMATSUKA MOE
Photographer: MAKIHARA SUSUMU
Styling & Hair and make-up: TOSHIKUNI ISAKO
Artist Management: SUGIMOTO TAKAMICHI (Bstar)
LOCATION COORDINATOR: OGAWA SHOJI (GUAM TV)
Art Director: MIZUKI RYOTA
Editor: SHIBATA HIROSHI (TAKESHOBO)

定価はカバーに表記してあります。

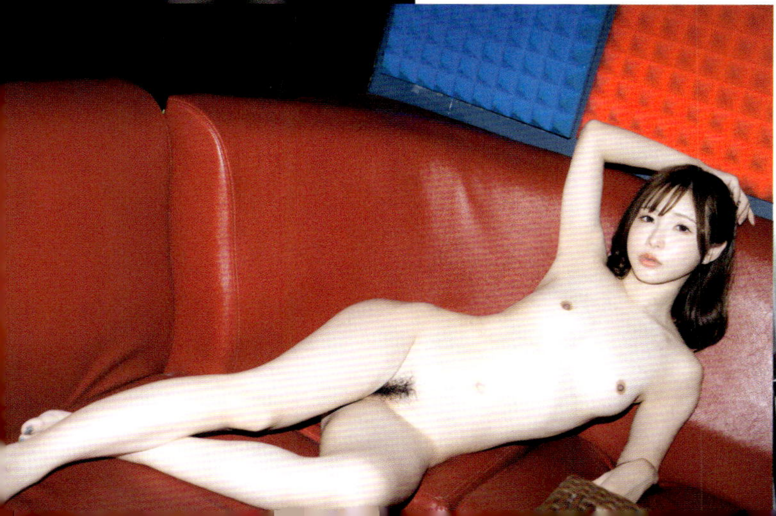